The King of Ing Wants to Sing

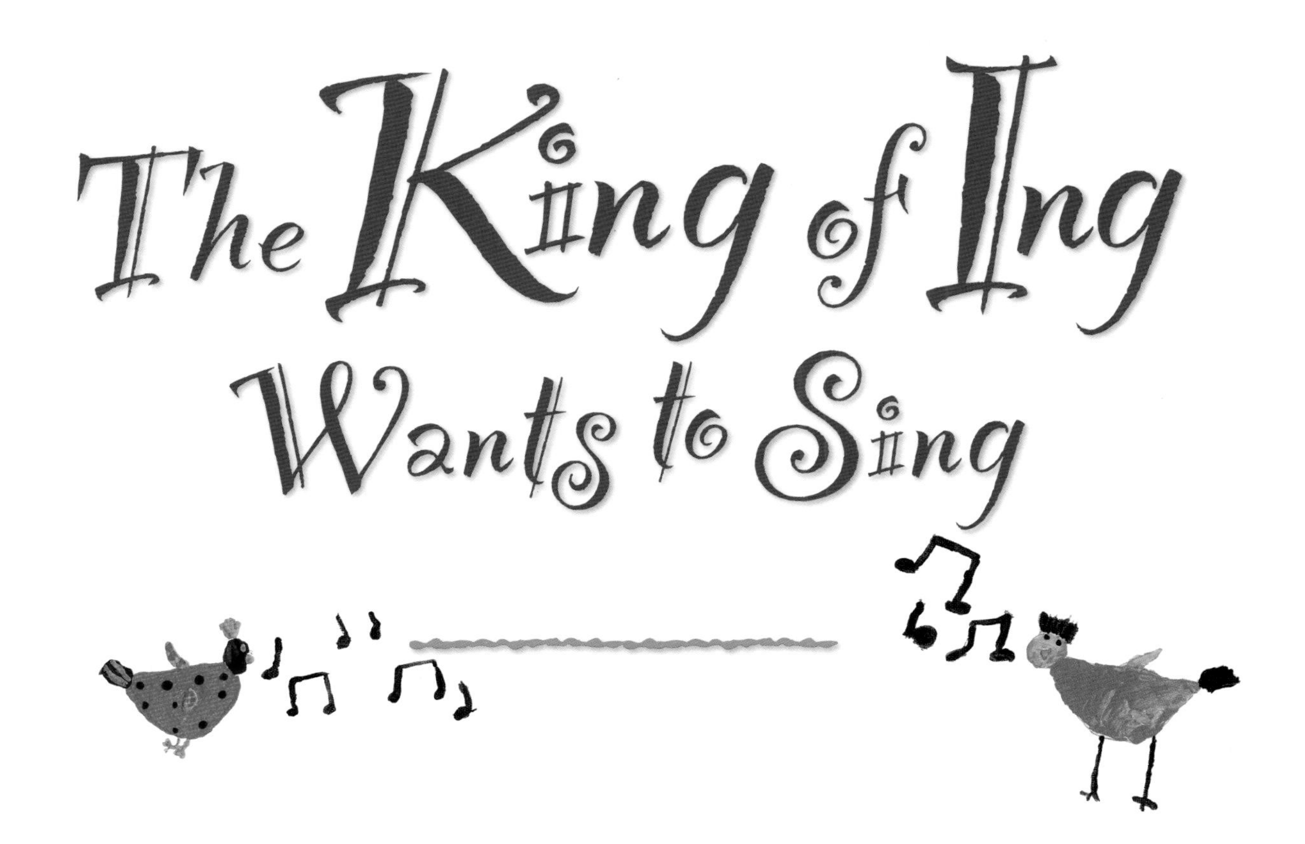

Written and Illustrated by Cindy Lou

Dedicated, with love, to
Michael and my two songbirds, Julia and Miah

Kite Tales Publishing, LLC
Milwaukee, Wisconsin
www.kitetalespublishing.com
www.thekingofing.com

ISBN 978-1-935332-00-8
Text and Illustrations by Cindy Lou
Book Design by David Cvetan
Printed by Color Express | cimarron

Printed in U.S.A.

There once lived a king
in the Kingdom of Ing.
He was crying.

Irving came running.
"Dear King of Ing, why are you crying?"

"I want to sing," said the King of Ing.
"Yet nothing makes me sing."

"I will bring something to make you sing," said Irving.
He set off to find something to make the King of Ing sing.

Kingdom of ING
Kingdom of ING
"It is of no use," said the King of Ing,
"for I have many things, yet no thing,
not a single thing, nothing makes me sing."

Irving came running.
"Dear King of Ing, I bring a ring for your finger.
Will you sing?"

The King of Ing put the ring on his finger.
He began crying.
"This ring for my finger does not make me sing."

"I will keep trying, dear King of Ing," said Irving.
"I will bring something to make you sing."

Kingdom of ING
Kingdom of ING
Kingd
"It is of no use," said the King of Ing,
"for I have many things, yet no thing,
not a single thing, nothing makes me sing."

Irving came running.
"Dear King of Ing, I bring a ming for your flower cuttings.
Will you sing?"

The King of Ing put his flower cuttings in the ming.
He began crying.
"This ming for my flower cuttings does not make me sing."

"I will keep trying, dear King of Ing," said Irving.
"I will bring something to make you sing."

"It is of no use," said the King of Ing,
"for I have many things, yet no thing,
not a single thing, nothing makes me sing."

Irving came running.
"Dear King of Ing, I bring a swing.
Will you sing?"

The King of Ing began swinging.
He began crying.
"This swing does not make me sing."

"I will keep trying, dear King of Ing," said Irving.
"I will bring something to make you sing."

Kingdom of ING
Kingdom of ING
Kingd
"It is of no use," said the King of Ing,
"for I have many things, yet no thing,
not a single thing, nothing makes me sing."

Irving came running.
"Dear King of Ing, I bring wings for flying.
Will you sing?"

The King of Ing put on the wings and was flying.
He began crying.
"These wings for flying do not make me sing."

"I will keep trying, dear King of Ing," said Irving.
"I will bring something to make you sing."

"It is of no use," said the King of Ing,
"for I have many things, yet no thing,
not a single thing, nothing makes me sing."

Irving came running.
"Dear King of Ing, I bring no thing, not a single thing, nothing.
But I will sing. Will you sing?"

The King of Ing began crying.

Irving began singing.

The King of Ing began listening.

Irving kept singing.

The King of Ing began trying.

Irving kept singing.

The King of Ing began humming.

Irving began smiling.

The King of Ing began singing!

Irving and the King of Ing were singing.

"No thing, not a single thing, nothing made me sing,"
sang the King of Ing, "I'm singing, thanks to Irving!"

The King of Ing